BRINGER OF THE RIVER WATERS

FORGOTTEN GODS: ORIGINS

LAURA GREENWOOD

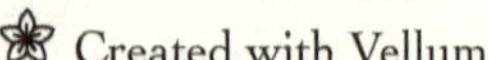 Created with Vellum

BLURB

When the river Nile doesn't flood like it's supposed to, the gods turn to hippo goddess, Taweret, to help with the problem.

Even with Taweret and Sobek's collective magic, they fail to find the problem, until they come across Isis on the side of the Nile.

Can they bring back the floods before it's too late?

Bringer Of The River Waters is a Forgotten Gods: Origins story which features Taweret and Sobek. It is based on myths from the New Kingdom of Ancient Egypt.

A NOTE ON THE GODS & GODDESSES OF THE FORGOTTEN GODS UNIVERSE

Due to the span of Ancient Egyptian history, many gods and goddesses took on multiple roles over the span of time (as demonstrated in The Queen Of Gods Mini-Series by Hathor's multitude of aspects). In most cases, the gods and goddesses in the fictional Forgotten Gods Universe have been given one of their various aspects. The family links the Ancient Egyptians formed between their gods weren't meant to represent blood family, but aspect ties. This is why many of the gods and goddesses are consorts with their siblings. In the context of the Forgotten Gods Universe, none of the gods are related to one another by blood, but many choose to create family bonds.

You can see a full list of Gods & Goddesses in

the Forgotten Gods Universe, as well as other definitions and information, on my website.

PROLOGUE

5 Years Ago...

The festival was in full swing, with gods and goddesses mingling with humans as they celebrated one thing or another. I'd lost track of what it's supposed to be for. That was always the case. A lot of the gods were still in the place where they were still trying to impress the humans, and that led to a lot of over the top celebrations. They weren't really my thing, but the younger gods seemed to like them.

"You look as if you want to be anywhere but here," Nut said as she came to stand next to me.

"Wouldn't you?"

A small smile lifted at the corners of her lips. "I can think of worse things to be doing with my time."

"Being cursed?"

"Precisely. I'd take a festival rather than that."

"You still haven't forgiven Ra for that, have you?" I asked.

"Would you?"

She had a point. Being cursed to be pregnant and unable to give birth took a toll on her, though she and Geb had found a solution with the help of a few other gods. I'd been lucky enough to be with her on the day she'd been able to give birth.

"I'm not sure I've forgiven him for what he did to you."

She chuckled. "It's been years, it might be time to."

"He hasn't forgiven us."

"That's because he's still worried about Osiris."

My gaze slipped over to where her eldest son was talking to his wife.

Osiris cut an imposing figure now that he was a grown man. I could see why Ra was worried about him. But that wasn't any excuse for what he'd done to Nut and Geb.

"I think Ra is just the kind of god who holds grudges regardless of if there's any reason to," I said.

"You might have a point there."

"Hopefully, it will blow over."

"He has been losing power ever since he lost control of Nehmetawy," Nut said.

"That's true. But that might only make him more reckless in his pursuit of power," I warned her.

She sighed and pushed a strand of dark hair out of her face. The glittering stars that dotted her dark blue skin shimmered even in the bright light of the sun.

In the distance, Geb waved towards us, beckoning for his wife to come join him.

"I need to go. But you should try to have fun, even if you don't want to be here."

"You know me so well."

"We've been friends for years, Taweret," Nut reminded me. "I'd like to think I know your likes and dislikes."

I smiled reassuringly at her. "True."

"So go, have some beer and celebrate whatever this is for."

"You don't know what it's for either?"

She laughed loudly. "I lost track a long time ago."

"Me too. But still try to make the most of it. I'll see you in a bit."

"Have fun with your husband," I told my friend.

"I always do."

She headed off in his direction, leaving me alone

to watch once more. Maybe she was right, I should get myself some beer and try to make the most of everything. I might not want to celebrate things the same way as some of the other gods did, but the festival was happening, I should take part.

I made my way over to the man handing out cups of beer. It wasn't anything fancy, mostly the same as we had with each of our meals, but it would be refreshing on a hot day.

"Thank you," I said as I took it from him and made my way further into the festival grounds.

No one stopped to talk to me, they were all too wrapped up in having a good time with their friends and loved ones. I didn't mind. If I could keep to myself for a while, it would get late enough that I could slip off and go do my own thing.

I headed towards the Nile. It was an almost certainty that there would be people celebrating there. At least that way I could get a shot of power from the river waters.

"Taweret, I didn't expect to see you today," a man said as I approached the bank.

My heart skipped a beat as I recognised Sobek. I'd always found him handsome but the glint in his eyes always made me wary. It probably wasn't his fault that he resembled the crocodiles he was linked

4

with. I was sure I resembled my sacred hippos to other people too.

"It is the festival..."

"You have no idea what it's for, do you?" he asked.

"Would you believe me if I said I did?"

A laugh boomed from the crocodile god. "No one has that good of a memory."

I flashed him a smile. "So, what are you doing here instead of at the main festival?"

"I suspect the same thing you are. Getting away from everyone and coming to the Nile for some peace."

Heat rose to my cheeks. Thank the river waters it wouldn't show on my face. "Am I that obvious?"

He shrugged. "I've noticed you don't seem to like many of the events. Especially since you lost Ra's favour."

"I don't think I had it to begin with," I pointed out.

"But you did cross him."

I sighed. "I wouldn't go that far. I helped Nut give birth, but that's my job."

"Ah, punished for something you should always have done. That sounds about right."

"I didn't ask for it," I muttered.

"I know. And for what it's worth, I don't think

it's right that you're being punished for something like this."

"Thanks, I appreciate it."

"So, did you want to go for a swim?" He gestured towards the river.

Indecision warred within me. Did I? Swimming in the Nile was always a pleasure for me, but it was something I'd always done alone, and I wasn't sure whether or not I wanted to change that. It felt like a deeply intimate activity and I barely knew Sobek other than a few conversations here and there during official functions.

"Not today," I said, hoping I wasn't going to come to regret it.

Sobek shrugged. "Perhaps another time."

"Maybe." I didn't want to promise anything I wasn't sure I'd be able to give. But with eternity stretched out before us, another time could mean anything from tomorrow, to three thousand years from now.

It would be interesting to see which it was.

ONE

BEING BANISHED WAS NO FUN. But then, I supposed that was the point. Despite how long it had been since I helped Nut give birth, I had to assume that was the reason behind Ra's choice. He wasn't the most rational of gods at the best of times, and when he was angry, that was even more true. I had no idea which deity I had to thank for this fit of anger, but I'd been the one who he'd chosen to take it out on. It was probably because Osiris had been named as the first Pharaoh. The power he had made Nut and Geb themselves untouchable, and considering Thoth had returned from Punt in a relationship with the extremely powerful Eye of Ra, I was the only one who had been involved in the whole affair who was easily punished at this point.

I gazed out onto the Nile, enjoying the sight of a baby hippo bouncing up and down next to its mother in the shallows. It wasn't quite big enough to keep its nose above the water by standing, which meant it had to do the cutest little hops to get air.

I knew Ra meant for this to be a punishment for me, but other than not seeing my friends as much as I'd want to, it wasn't too bad. And several of them had made an effort to come visit me. Hopefully in secret. I didn't want any of them getting into trouble for my sake.

Two hippos ran at one another, their huge mouths open and roaring. The sound was deafening. From this distance, I couldn't tell if it was to do with one of the female hippos, or if it was a territory dispute. And I wasn't about to try and get closer to find out. Only a fool would get in between fighting hippos.

I rose to my feet, deciding it was best if I left them in peace.

Darkness was starting to fall and a bright twinkle in the sky caught my attention.

I frowned and glanced back at the Nile. The inundation of the Nile should be happening and the waters should be flooding the banks and making them fertile for the year to come.

So why weren't they? I'd never known them to be this late before. While there wouldn't be any problems in the next couple of weeks or so, but after that...

A shudder ran down my spine. It wasn't worth thinking about what would happen if the flood didn't come.

The urge to try and do something about it surged through me, but I had to push it away. I wasn't in any kind of position to do anything. I couldn't even enter Egypt without causing more problems for myself.

Was this worth risking that?

My gaze tugged back to the hippos.

Yes.

There was no way around it. I needed to find out what was wrong with the Nile, or there'd be consequences none of us would like very much. Which meant heading back to Egypt, no matter what Ra decided to do to me as punishment. He'd never been very clear about that part.

I trekked away from my favourite spot by the river and headed towards the small hut I'd been calling home since I arrived in Nubia.

The moment the hut came into view, I did a double-take. There was someone waiting outside it pacing back and forth. I wasn't expecting anyone, was I? None of my friends had sent a messenger ahead, and they always did to make sure I wasn't taken off guard.

I approached cautiously. While whoever it was wouldn't be able to kill me, I could still get hurt, and I had no desire for that to be the case.

Once I was close enough to make out the man's features, relief flooded through me. I had no idea what Sobek was doing here, but I was reasonably certain he wasn't going to hurt me. I'd never even heard rumours of him raising his voice.

"Ah, you are here, I thought I was going to have to search the entirety of Nubia to find you," he said once I was in earshot.

I chuckled lightly. "I was by the river."

"That's probably where I should have started."

"Probably. Would you like to come inside for some wine while you tell me what you're here for?" I asked, gesturing towards my hut. "Before you get your hopes up, it's not a fancy vintage like you'd get at Karnak."

"I've had a long journey through the desert, anything you have is welcome."

"Why didn't you travel by the Nile?" I asked as I entered the hut with him following behind me.

"I didn't want to make the situation worse."

"You're here because of the floods," I surmised.

"How..."

"I have eyes." I filled two clay cups with wine and handed one of them to him.

Our fingers brushed as he took it and I glanced away, not wanting to see the intense expression in his eyes.

"I noticed it when I was by the Nile earlier. I saw the star and knew what it meant."

Sobek sighed. "I guess that makes my job easier."

"Did Ra send you?" I asked.

He shook his head. "He has absolutely no idea I'm here. He wasn't very interested in the problems with the Nile."

"Let's guess, he's still obsessed over Osiris being the Pharaoh and not wanting it to be the case."

"As far as I'm aware. I'm sure there's someone else who has annoyed him now."

"It's going to be a long forever if this is how he wants to keep playing it," I muttered.

A smirk lifted the corners of Sobek's lips. "I feel that's what everyone is worried about."

"Maybe he'll get bored. Eventually."

"We can hope."

I take a sip of my wine and sit on one of the reed mats. I rearrange my loose-fitting linen dress over my crossed legs to at least keep some semblance of modesty.

"What's this got to do with the Nile floods?" I asked. If that was really why he came, then he wasn't doing the best job at talking about it.

He sighed. "We were hoping you'd be able to help."

My eyebrows shot up. "With the floods?"

He nodded. "You're associated with the Nile..."

"Only very vaguely," I pointed out. "And not by magic." That wasn't my realm at all.

"But you feel at one with it, right? You feel something from the waters. I've seen it in your face."

I nodded slowly. "Yes. I feel at home there."

"Then I think you can help. Come to Shedet with me and help us work out what the problem is."

"You haven't specified who us is."

"Oh. Right. Hapi and I are working on the problem now, but if we can't figure out what the problem is, we were thinking that we could head to Elephantine and speak to the triad."

I nodded slowly. "I think we should go straight there," I admitted, grateful none of the plans involved going to Karnak. Elephantine was on the border between Nubia and Egypt, I could get away with going there without evoking Ra's anger. Shedet not so much. I wouldn't be able to feign innocence if I was found in Middle Egypt.

"Why do you think that?"

"There's more we can do with more help. Can you have Hapi meet us there?"

He nodded. "If we go down to the Nile, I'll send a crocodile with a message for him."

"That's a handy trick."

He grinned broadly, clearly pleased with himself. "Isn't it?"

"I wish I could do the same, the hippos are such grumps sometimes."

He snorted. "I can't imagine it would go down well with them to suggest taking a message to someone."

"If I ever pluck up the courage to try it, I'll make sure you're there."

His face lit up at the suggestion. "I'd like that."

"But now isn't the time. Especially not if we need to sort out the problems with the floods."

He sighed. "Sadly, there is no time to waste sitting around and drinking wine here."

"That's fine. There'll be better food and wine at Elephantine than I can provide, we'd both be much better there."

"Then we should get going. We can probably be

there by dawn." He was on his feet and brushing off his clothes within seconds.

The muscles of his torso rippled with each and every moment, making my mouth go dry. But I pushed all thoughts of Sobek's appearance out of my mind. We had a problem to solve, and that had to be our focus.

TWO

THE LUSH BANKS of Elephantine rose up from the middle of the Nile as we approached, with the sandstone temple peeking out from between the greenery. It was a majestic sight, and one I welcomed.

And not just because it meant I didn't have to return to Karnak any time soon. I'd be able to stay safe and out of Ra's way on this tiny island in the middle of the Nile. He'd probably have no idea I was even here.

A pair of crocodiles swam on either side of us, seeming to want to be close to Sobek. I'd never seen sacred animals behave that way before, hippos certainly didn't respond to me in the same way. Perhaps that was something I had to work on.

Another boat approached from afar. I had to

assume that one contained Hapi. I was reasonably sure that all of us would prefer not to put extra strain on the Nile by travelling via it, but when our destination was an island, there wasn't much choice.

Sobek grabbed one of the oars and used it to steer us up to a landing platform where a lone priest waited.

"Your Eminences, welcome to Elephantine. We're expecting you," he said, dipping his head to each of us in turn.

"Thank you," Sobek responded.

"If you'd allow me to take care of your boat, the lord and ladies of the island are waiting for you."

Sobek nodded and handed the oar to the priest before stepping off the boat. He held out his hand to me.

I wavered for a moment, unsure whether or not I should take it, but decided it would be rude not to. I doubted Sobek was trying to insinuate that I wasn't able to disembark by myself with the offer, he was simply being polite.

Carefully, I placed my hand on his and stepped onto the dock.

"If you head up the stairs and walk in the direction of the obelisk, you'll come to the right place," the priest instructed us. "I wish you a swift journey, Your Eminences."

He hopped onto the boat and began to steer it further into the island down a small canal.

"I haven't missed the formality of all this," I muttered.

"I'm not surprised, it can get tiring after a while."

We made our way up the stairs, neither of us saying much. I didn't want to admit it, but I was nervous about meeting Khnum again, and I'd never met either of the goddesses who completed the triad of Elephantine.

There weren't nearly as many priests and priestesses around as I was used to from living at Karnak, but that was a good thing, it definitely helped reassure me that Ra wasn't going to find out I was here. It was unlikely anyway, as the demi-gods tended to be loyal to the god they served, not the person who wanted to be in charge of us all.

The obelisk the priest had mentioned towered above the island, the shadow breaking up the brightness of the morning sun. Thankfully, it wasn't too hot yet, though perhaps the breeze from the Nile would help to keep the heat more palatable than some other places.

Three figures stood beneath it, waiting for us to arrive with an eerie stillness. The man in the middle was tall and broad, like most of the gods chose to look. The women on either side of him had the same elegance to them. The only way I was able to tell them apart from this distance was that the one on the left had lotus blossoms woven into her wig. From everything I'd heard, I had to assume that was Anuket, making the woman on the other side Satis.

It took everything I had not to brush down my simple dress and tidy up my hair. I often forwent a wig by choice, but having been in the Nubian wilderness for a while, my hair had grown a little unruly. Next to these goddesses, I didn't look like anyone important.

I supposed I could change that. We each had the ability to change our appearances to what we wanted them to be. Sometimes, there were certain things that were easier to keep in their natural form, like Nut's midnight blue skin, but others it was simple to change. My hair was one of the things about my physical appearance that I struggled with, hence why I didn't wear wigs very often and prefered a simple neat braid for formal occasions.

Khnum straightened as he saw us approach, which was impressive given how stiff he'd been before.

Perhaps he was as nervous as I was about the whole situation. I supposed this wasn't the most usual of circumstances with the Nile floods not coming as they should. We were all worried about that.

"Welcome to Elephantine," Khnum boomed. "I don't know if you've met my companions before, Taweret. This is Anuket and Satis."

I nodded to each of them in turn. "It's a pleasure to meet you."

"Likewise," Satis responded in a melodious voice.

"It's regrettable we're meeting under such trying circumstances," Anuket added.

"Is there anything you can tell us about the situation?" I asked, looking between the three gods.

Normally, we would spend more time on the pleasantries and the polite ways of greeting one another, but the situation was too dire for us to be wasting any time.

"Alas, we do not, " Khnum responded. "We hoped that with more Nile deities here, we might be able to solve the problem."

I nodded. "We can hope."

"I believe we saw Hapi's boat approaching as we docked," Sobek said.

Khnum nodded solemnly. "Once he has arrived, the six of us should share a meal and discuss what we might do. Until then, one of my priests will show you to your rooms. If you need anything, please let one of our attendants know."

"Thank you, it's appreciated." Perhaps the best thing for me to do was to take a swim in the Nile. This place was full of magic, perhaps it might tell me something about what the problem was.

Of course, that probably wouldn't work. If three powerful Nile gods like the triad couldn't figure out the problem, then what were the chances someone like me could.

Still, it was worth a try. They had to think I was useful for something, or none of them would have thought to seek me out.

Now I just needed to prove to the other gods that was a good decision.

THREE

THE COOL WATERS lap against my sun-warmed skin. On the one hand, it was glorious to be bathing in the Nile and to feel the power of the water throughout my entire body. On the other, it was more obvious than ever that something was seriously wrong. I couldn't put my finger on precisely what it was, but the river felt off.

How were we supposed to fix this when it wasn't obvious what the problem was?

Frustration welled up within me. As much as I tried to push it to the side so it didn't overwhelm me, I just couldn't find a way to. This felt impossible. And if we failed, there would be consequences for a lot of people. I didn't want to be around to witness that. Not when it would mean death and famine throughout the land.

We had to fix this, there wasn't an alternative.

Something changed in the water. I stood up, rivulets running down my skin and splashing back into the river as I turned around.

The reeds on the bank shifted against one another as someone moved through them.

I relaxed when I noticed Sobek heading towards me and sank back down to cover my nakedness beneath the surface. I normally didn't mind people seeing me like this, but for some reason, being around him made me feel more self-conscious than anyone else.

He smiled at me, but I could tell from the tightness in his eyes that he didn't like the way the Nile felt either.

"I thought I heard someone out here," he said as he waded over to join me.

"I figured the easiest way to try and work out what's wrong with the Nile is to come and be one with it."

He nodded. "That makes sense. Any luck?"

"You know the answer to that," I muttered darkly.

Sobek sighed. "I do. I don't want to, but I do."

He stood close to me, his feet touching the bottom this close to the bank. I could have gone out deeper into the river, but hadn't wanted to in case Hapi's arrival meant I was needed on land.

"And that's just it. Everything about this feels wrong, but I can't figure out why. I've not encountered anything like this before." A shiver ran down my spine.

The water sloshed as Sobek lifted an arm and placed it around me in a gesture of comfort. He tugged me closer, until I could feel his body heat even through the cool water.

While I did feel reassured, all I could really think about was the fact we were both naked. I had no idea where this kind of thought was coming from, I'd seen plenty of people without clothes on, both male and female, and none of them had made me feel as aware of it as he did.

"What are we going to do?" I whispered.

"About the Nile, I don't know," he admitted.

A frown tugged at my face. "But you do about something else?" Maybe I'd misheard him, but there'd definitely been some kind of implication in his tone, I was sure of it.

"I know what to do about us," he said softly.

My eyes widened and I reached up to brush a strand of hair out of my eyes just for something to do.

"Us?" I squeaked.

He searched my face, probably looking for some kind of sign that I wasn't completely surprised by his statement.

"Yes, us."

"There isn't an us," I pointed out slowly.

To my surprise, Sobek laughed lightly. "Of course there isn't yet. But that doesn't mean there can't be."

"Oh." My heart skipped a beat. Which he could probably feel thanks to our proximity to one another.

Great. There wasn't going to be any hiding the effect he was having on me then.

"If you want there to be?"

Without realising what I was doing, I found myself nodding.

His small smile turned into a grin. "Can I kiss you?"

Heat rose to my cheeks as I considered the question. Should I let him? It wasn't like I hadn't thought about it before.

"Yes." The word came out stronger than I'd expected it to, almost as if my mind was already made up, it just hadn't had a chance to express itself yet.

He leaned in and my eyes fluttered closed. His

hot breath fanned against my lips, increasing my anticipation for what was to come.

His lips brushed against mine, gentle and searching as he made sure I was on board with what he was doing.

I was. And I needed him to know that.

I wrapped my arms around his neck and pulled him closer. The hard planes of his body pressed against me, only serving to make the kiss more exciting.

The river washed against us, adding a serene note that made the rest of the world almost disappear completely. I could still sense that something was wrong with it, but for the first time today, it could wait. Not for long, but I needed some time to deal with everything going on. I wanted to make the most of whatever was happening between me and Sobek.

We broke apart, staring at one another with an intensity that couldn't be feigned.

"Are you all right?" He reached up and brushed away the same strand of hair that had been annoying me earlier.

"More than all right," I admitted.

"I've wanted to do that for a long time, but you never seemed to want to be alone with me."

I squeaked. "That's because I was worried about what I might say or do."

He chuckled, the sound going right through me. "So instead, we avoided one another and lost some time."

"Maybe a couple of years at most. That's not long in the grand scheme of things."

"I suppose that's true," he agreed. "You could easily get sick of me well before that."

"I can't make any promises. Eternity is a long time."

He grimaced and panic flooded through me. Had I misjudged the situation? I cursed myself for thinking I could do this kind of jesting. I wasn't very good at it. One of the side effects of being a goddess of childbirth, it was much more likely that I would be needed to speak candidly than in riddles.

"Eternity sounds like a long time when you put it like that."

"In relationship terms?"

"In any terms," he corrected. "I don't have any commitment issues, I promise. It's just that sometimes I find it overwhelming to think that we have an eternity of life still to live."

"Oh, I see."

"I promise, it's not about you. You know how it is. This is the job we're expected to do for the rest of our very long lives, and sometimes, it's overwhelming to think that."

I reached out and placed a reassuring hand on his arm. "I know what you mean."

"You would make it less daunting," he admitted softly.

"You don't know that. Maybe I'll break your heart in a hundred years or so."

"I hope you don't, but it's a risk I'm willing to take if you are."

I nodded. "I am."

"Good." He pulled me back to him and kissed me again.

I melted into his arms, enjoying his touch and the way it made me feel. If he kept doing this, then I doubted I'd be breaking his heart any time soon. I certainly wouldn't be doing it on purpose. I wouldn't want to hurt anyone if I knew that I was doing it.

I lost myself in his arms for a while longer. We couldn't stay away from the others for too long or they'd come looking for us, but at least the two of us were able to take a break for a short amount of time. Hopefully, once we'd solved the problem with the Nile, we'd be able to spend some time just the two of us.

Preferably far away from Karnak and Ra's potential wrath.

FOUR

IT TURNED out that none of the others had any ideas about what was causing the problems with the Nile either. Which was not a good situation for the six of us to be in. Hapri had even frowned, which was almost unheard of from the god. Up until this point, I hadn't even realised he was capable of being sad, jovial was his middle name.

Or it would be if any of us had middle names.

I moved through the depths of the Nile, using the bottom of the riverbed to push myself along in my hippo form. I hated the inability to swim, but I couldn't match the speeds I could manage by running and bouncing along the sandy bottom of the river in this form.

Above me, Sobek weaved through the water with the immense grace of a crocodile. The others were all going in different directions to check for other problems. Anuket was heading towards the cataracts she was the goddess of by the Nubian borders, while Khnum and Satis were checking the left bank as we searched the right. With the different speeds we could all travel, it made sense for us to split up instead of travelling together. We'd be able to send messengers to one another if we found anything that needed everyone's attention.

So far, it had been another dead end. There was nothing that would help us get to the bottom of what was stopping the Nile from flooding the way it should.

We carried on the same way we had for the last ten miles, not coming any closer to an answer. We should stop and rest soon, it wouldn't be good if we let ourselves become overtired, especially if we needed magic in order to bring about the floods.

After a while, Sobek indicated to something on the bank with his snout.

I didn't need telling twice. Partly because we'd never be able to understand each other while we were in these forms.

I pushed with my back foot and used the momentum to propel myself towards the surface.

Water rushed past my ears, roaring almost as loudly as I could if I felt like it.

I broke through the surface of the river, the water running over my nose and making my appearance suitably dramatic.

Sobek was already standing on the edge of the Nile, already in his human form. I had to admit to being a little jealous about how easily he could turn while swimming. I was graceful under the water, but it wasn't anything like what he could do.

Once I was shallow enough to be more efficient in my human form, I called it to the surface, forgetting for a moment that my dress would get wet. It wouldn't matter for long, the sun was beating down with the intense heat that only came from the middle of the day.

"Is it time to take a break?" I asked him.

He shook his head. "I heard something. Can't you?"

I cocked my head to the side and strained my ears. Sure enough, the sound of muffled anguish greeted me through the reeds.

"What is it?"

"I've no idea. But we should go find out. Even if it's nothing to do with the river, it would be good for us to help."

I nodded, affection for him surging through me. I liked that he wanted to help someone, even if he had no idea who they were.

We moved towards the sounds, which increasingly sounded like crying. Discomfort settled within me. I had no idea who it was, but they were clearly in a great amount of pain. And if I was judging it right, it was emotional and not physical.

Somehow, that was worse.

I swallowed down my nerves about what we were going to find. It wasn't going to be good, whatever we found.

A woman leaned over a prone form weeping uncontrollably. Bright red splotches covered the ground next to her. I hoped her husband hadn't been attacked by one of our sacred animals, we might not be the people she wanted to see if that was the case.

Hopefully, she wouldn't be able to recognise us.

She shifted and looked up to face us. I gasped.

Isis. What was she doing all the way out here? Shouldn't she be back at Karnak doing all the things a queen should?

Horror settled within me as I realised that must mean the man at her side was Osiris. I knew they'd had a rocky start to their marriage, but they'd fallen deeply in love after a while.

"Taweret?" She sniffed and wiped her nose with her arm.

"What happened?" I asked, trying not to let the

pain I was feeling at the sight enter my voice. She didn't need that making things worse.

I sank to my knees next to her, resisting the urge to pull her into my arms and offer her comfort.

"Seth." She spat the name with more venom than I thought she was capable of.

"What did he do?"

Sobek shifted uncomfortably behind us, but stayed silent. He'd clearly worked out that the two of us knew one another well enough to be having this conversation.

"He..." Isis took a deep breath to steady her nerves. "He tricked Osiris into getting into the perfect sized box and then he killed him." She bit her lip.

"Oh."

"But he wouldn't let me have the body. He cut him into fourteen pieces and scattered them around Egypt. This is all I've managed to find so far." She gestured to the body next to his.

It was only then I noticed the mess it was in. What I'd mistaken for blood was actually parts of Osiris' innards spilling out from the large wounds on his torso. I held my breath as I counted the pieces.

Ten. She was still missing four pieces to make her husband whole so he could be buried.

"Do you know where Seth scattered them?" Sobek asked, stepping forward.

She shook her head. "I think in the Nile, but I'm not sure."

"We can search for them for you," I promised without thinking. Our own quest would have to wait. Perhaps it was Seth's betrayal of his brother that had caused the problems with the Nile in the first place, that was often how these things worked.

"We will," Sobek promised, placing his hand on my shoulder.

"Do you have someone who can stay with you and help put him back together?" I asked.

Isis nodded. "Nephthys is searching at the moment." She pointed to the sky and understanding dawned on me. The sisters had been using their other forms to look for pieces of Osiris from above.

I was glad she had Nephthys to help her.

If only it had done the same for Osiris and Seth. They saw one another as brothers, but jealousy had turned them against one another. Seth was the only god I knew who could match Ra for pettiness.

And this time he'd gone too far. I wouldn't be surprised if many of the gods and goddesses never forgave him for this. He's certainly made an enemy of Isis.

"If you're all right here, then we'll go look," I said.

Isis nodded and took my hand in hers. "Thank you."

"Always. I helped bring you into this world, I'm not about to abandon you now."

She managed a weak smile.

My heart ached for her. I knew she wasn't, but she looked so young and helpless when she gazed up at me with her eyes watering and pain etched into her features. I wished I could make things easier for her and take away some of the horror of the situation, but that wasn't possible. She'd have to live with the soul-crushing events, even if it was going to be awful for her. But she had a lot of friends back at Karnak who could help her through it, and I would too if I was able to.

I rose to my feet and said a quick goodbye, hating that I had to leave her, but knowing it was probably better for her if I searched for the parts of Osiris that were missing, it would give her peace of mind.

I hoped.

Sobek and I headed back to the river, neither of us saying a word. Seth's actions were still sinking in, and I hated the thought of what he'd done.

"Should we alert the others?" he asked once we

were standing in the shallows with the water lapping at our lower legs.

I sighed. "Their help would be good, and hopefully make the search shorter, but should we really pull them away from the Nile problem?"

"I don't know," he admitted. "A part of me thinks this is linked."

"How would that even be possible?"

"I honestly have no idea. It's a gut feeling."

I nodded. "I got that too, back there when Isis was talking to us. Magic works in mysterious ways."

"You sound like Heka."

"I'd have to get a lot more mysterious to sound like him," I pointed out.

The god of magic and medicine was renowned for being hard to understand. It made having a conversation with him almost impossible.

"We should tell them," I said firmly. "They'll be able to help, even if it's just by keeping an eye out while they're searching for the issue with the river. We can tell them that we have a hunch that it's all connected, but we don't know for sure, then we're being honest with everyone."

He nodded and whistled.

Three crocodiles appeared as if from nowhere and came right up to us. Their tails swished back and forth in the water, but I already knew they weren't going to hurt us.

Sobek crouched down and touched their heads one by one.

I raised an eyebrow, not having expected the messages to work that way. But sure enough, the crocodiles swam off in the direction of the gods they were delivering messages to.

"All right. That should be done. Now we can focus on our part of the search."

"I hope we're successful." I tried not to think about how much more heartbroken Isis would be if we weren't. It wasn't worth thinking about.

Sobek reached out and took my hand in his, giving it a squeeze. "We'll do everything we can to make sure we're successful."

"Seth is devious..."

"But he didn't have help," he pointed out. "Isis does. Lots of it. We'll make sure she's triumphant."

"I hope you're right."

"Me too."

I swallowed down my nerves and changed into my hippo form, unable to voice any of my other thoughts. There would be plenty of time for that once we'd performed the proper funeral rites for Osiris.

FIVE

THE TREK back to Isis with the twelfth piece of Osiris' body was almost as bad as the first time we came upon her. I hated having to deliver the dismembered part of his body to her. Especially when each time her face showed more and more pain.

Her loss wasn't getting any easier for her. She was strong, but this had pushed her too far. I wished I could change it for her, but I knew it was too late.

A screech drew my attention to the sky where a large bird swooped down. Even before she'd landed, Nephthys transformed herself back into her human form, though she still had huge black wings sprouting from her back. I had no doubt she was going straight back into the air once she'd talked to us. The bags under her eyes revealed how tired she was.

"Did you..." She nodded to the reed basket I was carrying with all the reverence I had.

I nodded.

She let out a relieved sigh. "That's thirteen."

"Someone else found one? I thought this was twelve," Sobek said.

Nephthys nodded. "Hapi came across a piece and brought it to us this morning. Is it..." she trailed off.

"Is it what?" I asked, confusion coming over me.

"Is it his manhood?"

I startled, not having expected that to be her question.

"No, should it be?" Sobek asked.

Nephthys shook her head. "There's a spell I found, I'm not sure if it will work, but it includes making him a new one and it might put his ka to rest after what's been done to it."

My eyebrows shot up. "Are you sure that's a real thing? Heka might have been playing an inappropriate trick on you."

"I don't think so," she assured me. "He'd never do that to me."

Huh. Interesting. I didn't realise there was anything between them. She was technically married to Seth, but it wasn't a happy marriage and if recent events were anything to go by, I didn't imagine she'd be very happy going back to him. I certainly wouldn't if I found myself in Nephthys' position.

"It's worth a try," Sobek said, being a little more diplomatic than I had.

I nodded in agreement despite my reservations. There wasn't any harm in trying it. The worst thing that would happen was nothing. Isis would still be heartbroken, but it wouldn't be worse than it already was.

"I'll meet you at the temple," she said, already beating her wings. I guessed we weren't actually getting a choice in that part.

She lifted herself into the sky, shrinking and transforming as she did.

"I always envied her grace," I muttered as I watched her fly inland.

"You don't need to..."

"Pfft. You've seen me change forms, right?"

"Well, yes."

"There's nothing graceful about that."

"There is," Sobek assured me. "Especially when you're under the water and moving. You're amazing to watch."

"Thank you," I mumbled, staring at the ground,

not wanting him to sense my embarrassment at the compliment. "You're very graceful too."

He grinned. "That's the predator in me."

"I like it," I admitted. "But should we be talking like this when..." I nodded towards the basket, not wanting to voice the words.

A guilty expression that mirrored how I felt crossed Sobek's face. At least he seemed to feel the same way I did.

"Maybe not."

We walked the rest of the way in silence, both of us a little uncomfortable now we'd had the realisation over what we were escorting to Isis.

As soon as we approached the temple, Isis came outside to greet us, with Nephthys following right behind. At least that explained how she knew we'd arrived, otherwise, it could be a little disconcerting.

"You found the thirteenth piece?" she whispered.

I nodded and held out the basket to her.

Slowly she reached out and took it from me, a heartbroken expression on her face.

We followed her back inside to where Osiris was lying on a mummification table, mostly together save for the two missing pieces. Not that one of them was particularly noticeable, given what it was. I had to wonder why Seth had gone to the trouble of cutting off his manhood specifically. Perhaps he thought it had some kind of magical powers. I wasn't sure and I didn't want to ask.

Isis set down the basket and reverently lifted the lower leg from it. She slotted it into place and took a needle and thread. With deft fingers, she reattached the leg to Osiris until he was complete again. Well, almost.

She finished and stepped back, a shudder running through her as she looked on. A single tear rolled down her cheek. "I thought something would happen," she admitted.

"Will you let me try something, sister?" Nephthys asked.

Isis nodded. "Do you need me to stay?"

"No."

She took a shaky breath and left the temple.

"Would the two of you mind leaving too?" Nephthys asked.

"Of course. Let us know if you need anything."

"I will." She turned her attention to Osiris and started to mutter something under her breath. Presumably, the words of the spell Heka had told her to use. I still wasn't convinced it was going to work, but if she wanted to try, then I wasn't about to stop her.

We left the mortuary temple and followed Isis

down to the bank of the Nile. She stared off into space, not seeming to be responsive at all.

"I'm sorry," I said to her as I took a seat next to her.

"I don't know what I was thinking," she whispered. "I thought sewing the last piece of him together would do something."

"Did anyone tell you it would?"

"No." A fat tear splashed on the ground by her feet. "It was a foolish dream that I could see him again."

"You might be able to. We're not supposed to be able to die."

She gave a bitter laugh. "You know that's a lie, right?"

"What?" I blinked a few times, trying to process what she was saying.

"Only some people know, and we're not supposed to tell others, but all of us can die. We have to be killed in a very specific way, and nobody is aware of most of them. But we can die."

"And Seth somehow managed to figure out how Osiris was able to?" The disbelief came through Sobek's words stronger than I expected it to be.

Isis smothered a sob. "Someone who knew probably told him."

My heart sank. There were very few people who

would do that. And if the fact gods could die was something only known by a few, it made the pool smaller still.

"Do you have any suspicions?"

Isis shook her head. "But for all we know, Seth tricked them into revealing it. You know what he's like. He can be charming when he wants to be."

Her tears came faster, making her voice thick. They rolled down the bank, shimmering as they went and catching my attention in the process. They shouldn't be visible. The earth around the river banks was already drying up, they should have absorbed the tears as the only water they'd had in a few weeks.

Isis' tear reached the Nile and caused a ripple effect out from it.

"Sobek," I whispered, my voice barely audible over Isis' sobs.

"Magic," he whispered.

"Heka knows what he's doing sometimes."

"You think this was his doing?" I asked, not convinced. I hadn't seen Heka since leaving Karnak, and he wasn't big on leaving his workrooms. He liked to spend his time researching and perfecting his medicines.

"You don't?"

"Why don't you go and investigate the river, I'll stay here with Isis."

He nodded and rose to his feet.

"What's happening?" the other goddess said through her sobs.

"The Nile didn't flood a few weeks ago as it should."

Alarm crossed her face. "Why didn't you tell me?"

"You had other things to worry about, and we were searching for the cause."

"Do you think it's me?" she whispered. "I'm not a Nile goddess."

"You're not," I agreed. "But your tears are doing something to the water."

Sobek pushed through the reeds to get back to us. "The river is responding." His excitement was clear in his eyes, but he tried to keep his expression sombre for Isis' benefit. "I think if we go down to the river to guide the magic, we might be able to influence it enough to bring the flood."

Relief travelled through me. That was good news. Definitely the best we'd had recently.

"What do I need to do?" Isis asked, glancing between us.

"Cry out your pain," I told her. "Everything. All

the frustration, anger, mourning. Let it all out and we'll do the rest."

She smiled weakly. "I have plenty of that."

"Tell us if it gets too much for you, or if we pull too much magic," I said.

She nodded, but I knew without her saying anything that she wasn't going to do that. She'd see this through until the floodwaters rushed through or we stopped. I'd have to keep a close eye on her to make sure she wasn't giving too much.

I approached the water with caution, unsure what to make of the situation. I'd never heard of anything like this before, but magic worked in mysterious ways. I wasn't going to turn my back on it just because I couldn't make sense of what I was seeing.

The moment I dipped my foot in the water, I felt the difference. The river was singing in response to Isis' tears.

"Do you have any idea what we're supposed to do?" I asked Sobek.

"No."

"That's a good start," I muttered.

"I think we just need to guide the tears into the water. That way they can do what they need to."

"All right. Let's do this." I sank down beneath

the surface, staying in my human form so I could keep half an eye on Isis.

She seemed to have taken our instructions to heart, and the tears were falling faster than they had before. Or maybe she just felt like she could cry now that she was alone. Ish.

I opened myself up to the magic, feeling it play in the currents of the water. I barely paid any attention to Sobek who floated a few feet away doing the same thing as I was.

The river pulsed and danced, taking every bit of magic Isis' tears brought with them. I had no idea why this was working, or how, but I could tell that it was.

I had no idea how long the two of us stayed submerged in the water making the transition easier for the Nile, but eventually, the magic faded.

The river didn't go back to the way it had felt before, reassuring me that things really had been fixed. At least for now. We might have to do more later, but this was a good start.

I glanced back to the bank to check on Isis, but she was already gone. No doubt she was rushing back to her husband and sister. I didn't blame her. I wouldn't like the idea of losing Sobek, and we'd only been together for a few weeks. Isis and Osiris had been through so much together already.

"Should we go back to the temple?" he asked, drawing my attention away from my thoughts.

I shook my head. "Let's give them some time. We should enjoy the river now it feels like it should again."

"The Nile, or one another?" he asked, reaching out and pulling me to him.

His lips were on mine within an instant, and I melted into him, enjoying his touch in a way I hadn't been able to before. The floods were coming. We'd done it.

SIX

MY HEART SANK as we headed back to the mortuary temple. While the river returning to normal was a good thing, it didn't erase the pain Isis was going through. And while I was sure she was glad she'd managed to help all her people, it meant next to nothing next to the loss of her husband.

My heart went out for her. And for Nut and Geb. I was sure my friends would have heard about the death of their son. They might not have been related to him by blood, but they'd certainly treated one another like a family.

Yet another reason it was so strange Seth had turned against his brother. Nut and Geb had always made sure he wanted for nothing.

Sobek brushed a hand against my lower back. I leaned into him, glad I didn't have to go through all of this alone. That would be even worse than the situation already was.

"Did you send crocodiles to the others?" I asked, mostly for something to say, I was certain he'd already done it. That task couldn't wait.

"I did. But I don't think they'll need telling, they'll be able to feel the difference in the Nile like we can."

I nodded.

A screech announced Nephthys before she did. This time, she changed all the way into her human form without her wings. She must mean business.

"Anubis is on his way," she said solemnly.

I nodded. That was good news. Or good-ish news. With his help, we should be able to perform the death rites we needed for Osiris to be whole in the next life.

A loud scream came from inside the table.

We exchanged worried looks and rushed inside, desperate to discover what the problem was so we could help.

My eyes widened as I took in Osiris sitting on the mummification table.

Very much alive.

I wasn't the only one. Nephthys froze where she was standing, clearly very confused by the whole situation. I guessed her spell hadn't worked, then.

"What happened?" she asked.

"That's not something I have the answer to," Isis admitted, her voice shaking ever so slightly.

"And what happens now?" Nephthys asked.

Isis turned her attention back to her husband. "You can reclaim the throne from Seth and put everything right," she suggested.

"I can't." Sadness crept into his expression at the words. "I died. I can't remain in the land of the living."

My heart ached for the two of them. It was cruel for Isis to have seen him awake only for them not to be together. I wished there was something we could do for them.

"But I can journey to Duat and become the ruler of the dead. I can serve my purpose there just as I can on Earth."

Isis nodded. "I wish you could stay here."

"I know," he acknowledged. "I feel the same. But I will be able to visit. As will you."

"What do we do about your brother?" Nephthys asked, worry tainting every part of her question. She was still Seth's wife, which meant she was still under his control while he had power.

"While there's nothing I can do, Isis will soon have a child who will be able to defeat him and take the throne," Osiris announced.

Isis stared at her husband in disbelief. It must be news to her.

Osiris chuckled, then reached out his hand, placing it gently on Isis' belly. "Soon, my love."

"I hope you're right," Isis said.

I stepped back into Sobek, trying not to feel too much like I was intruding on an intimate moment. I doubted either of them even realised we were here.

"I am. I've seen what will pass, and am sure that is what it will be. Our son will be born, and with your love and protection, he'll grow into the strong leader our people need."

"I hope so," she whispered.

I did too. I hadn't been around for any of Seth's reign, having been banished by Ra and then distracted by the Nile, but from what others had said, it hadn't been good for anyone.

"We should go," Sobek whispered.

I nodded. I didn't want to intrude on the reconciled lovers any longer than I had to.

Neither of us said anything as we slipped out of the door. Even from this distance, the river was calling to us, and I couldn't wait to get back into it.

Sobek caught my hand in his and entwined his fingers with mine.

"Wait!" Isis shouted.

We turned around to find her running towards us.

She flung her arms around my neck and held me tightly. "Thank you so much."

"I didn't do anything," I pointed out.

"You don't know that. When I left earlier, my husband was dead. You did whatever it was with the river, and now he isn't."

"I don't think they're linked," I assured her.

She pulled back, an emotional smile on her face. "Maybe not, but in my mind they are. So thank you, both."

"I'm always here if you need me, just send me a message and I'll be there, you know that."

"I do. Thank you."

"You've said that already," I pointed out.

"And I'll say it a thousand times again. Maybe I should organise a festival for you..."

Sobek chuckled. Probably knowing exactly how I'd feel about that.

"No, please don't. They're not my thing."

"Hmm. All right, but maybe a festival to celebrate the floods. Everybody would like that."

"They probably would," I agreed.

She nodded. "That's what we'll do. You'll come, won't you?"

"I'm not sure I'll be able to," I admitted. "I

shouldn't even be here, Ra banished me." I was surprised she'd forgotten.

"Ah. Right. I'll see if we can do something about that. I'll send a messenger to you soon?"

I nodded, not really minding if she didn't.

"Go spend time with your husband," I urged her. "Make the most of your second chance."

"And your baby," Sobek added.

She touched her stomach, still surprised at the words. "It's going to take some getting used to."

I chuckled. "Your mother said the same. But just like I helped her, when your time comes, I'll do everything I can to help you too."

"Thank you, Taweret. For everything."

"And that's enough thanks," I half-scolded, feeling weird for talking to one of the most powerful goddesses in existence this way.

"Sorry, I'll try and remember."

"I'd like that. I'll see you soon."

She waved as she ran back to the mortuary temple.

I shook my head in bemusement.

"It sounds like you have her undying gratitude," Sobek said, wrapping me in his arms.

"It seems like it." I twisted around so I could look up at him. "So, what now?"

"We should head back to Elephantine so we can

fill the others in on everything that's happened. And after that, how would you like to come back to Shedet with me?"

My mouth fell open. "I can't, I'm..."

"Banished, yes, I know. But Ra never visits. He won't even know you're there. You can take advantage of the Nile and watch the family of hippos that have made one of the temple lakes their home.

"Oh, now you're playing dirty."

"If it gets you to agree, then it's worth it."

I let out a light laugh. "Fine. But if I hear that Ra is going to visit, I'm out of there really fast."

"I'll protect you if he does," Sobek promised. "And we'll work on getting you back in his good graces."

"I don't need his good graces, just his non-banishing ones."

"Then that's what we'll try and achieve."

"Thank you, I appreciate it."

"Didn't you just tell Isis off for saying that?"

I groaned. "Because it was constant, not because she was wrong to do it. And I can't believe I did that, she's the queen."

"And you were there when she was born, I don't think her status in life matters too much then."

"You might be right about that."

"I'm right about a lot of things," he countered.

"Hmm. We'll see about that. But come on, we should get going. If the others have received your message already, they'll probably be on their way to the island."

He nodded. "I know this wasn't the easiest few weeks, but I'm glad we got a chance to spend time together."

"Me too." The words were more true than anything I'd said in my life. They rang out through the air, reverberating with the promise of what was to come.

SEVEN

THE SETTING SUN sent ripples of colour across the surface of the Nile, only emphasising the shadows of the palm trees more.

It was beautiful.

Beyond beautiful, even. I was glad Sobek had asked me to come here, especially as I didn't have a cult centre of my own. I didn't need it when I was a deity to every household throughout Egypt.

The family of hippos he'd promised me played in the shallows, emerging from the deep waters now some of the heat of the day had started to dissipate. I smiled at the sight. They only added to the perfection of the view. As did the crocodiles that congregated around the whole place. Shedet was truly Sobek's home.

I leaned back into him, pleased to be able to

spend some time together. Since returning, he'd been understandably busy getting everything back in order after his absence. I'd probably have had to do something similar at my temple within the Karnak complex if I wasn't still banished. And if Isis ever managed to get her way, I would be doing just that once this farce ended. There was clearly nothing tangible stopping me from setting foot in Egypt or I wouldn't be here. Shedet might be secluded, but it was also in the middle of the country. Some people might say I was tempting fate. But I refused to believe that.

"Your Eminences," a priest I vaguely recognised said.

"What is it, Abasi?" Sobek asked.

Ah. That was his name. I should start trying to remember what each of the priests was called, but Sobek had so many that it was hard to keep up.

"I have a scroll for you," he said, holding it out.

"Thank you." Sobek took it from him. "Is there anything else?"

Abasi shook his head.

"Then that'll be all."

"Your Eminences." Abasi dipped his head to each of us in turn before disappearing back in the direction of the main temple complex.

"What is it?" I asked Sobek.

"I'm not sure, it's for you." He handed me the scroll of papyrus and waited for me to open it, being careful to look away so he didn't intrude on anything private.

I unroll it and scan the elegant hieroglyphics written across the page in handwriting I remembered well. "It's from Isis," I told him.

"Oh? Is everything all right?"

I nodded. "She says that Osiris is settling into the underworld well and the two of them have already found ways for it to work. It seems that he can exist here without much problem, but he can only rule in Duat."

"That's good for them," Sobek acknowledged.

"It is. She says the baby is kicking and they're still arguing about what to call him."

Sobek chuckled. "Won't the baby be a god?"

"I assume so. There haven't been many goddesses who have given birth yet, so it's hard to tell."

"Why do they even need to if the children that come from the process aren't related to them?" he asked.

I shrugged. "That's something I've been trying to answer ever since Nut got pregnant, but there truly doesn't seem to be an answer beyond that's the way it is. I suppose we could ask the same about whatever method the rest of us used to come into being."

"That's fair."

"It is."

"Any news on your banishment?" he prompted.

"Erm..." I scanned down the page. She'd managed to cram a lot of news onto a reasonably small piece of papyrus, it was hard not to miss anything. "Yes, here. She says that my banishment has been lifted and I can return to Karnak. After hearing how I'd helped Isis and Osiris, Ra had no way of being able to uphold it without making himself look bad. Though she also says that he's mostly doing it to save face as he's starting to realise he doesn't have as much power as he once did."

Sobek snorted. "Unsurprising."

"I don't think Ra's realised that if he's nice to people, it'll get him much further than it does now."

"That's definitely not something he's learned yet."

"Maybe one day," I said.

"I wouldn't hold your breath."

"I'm very good at that, though. An advantage of being able to change forms into a hippo," I pointed out.

A bemused smile crossed his face. "Even so, I wouldn't advise it."

"Oh, I know. Waiting for Ra on anything would be a waste of time."

"Is there anything else?"

I nodded. "She invites us to the first annual Wafaa El-Nil festival next year to celebrate the flooding of the Nile."

"She actually did that?" Surprise echoed through his voice.

"Did you really think she wouldn't?"

"I don't know her very well, everything I do know about her is from hearsay."

"Ah, well Isis doesn't say things she doesn't mean. She was perfect for the role of queen, just like Osiris was for the position of Pharaoh. I fear what will happen next with them gone from their positions." I tried not to let the thoughts overwhelm me.

"Their son will do exactly what Osiris said he would. He'll grow up strong and take the throne back from Seth."

"I hope he grows up fast," I muttered.

"He will. He's a god, for a start. But he's also needed. You know how that goes."

"I do," I admitted.

"It might take some time for the balance of power to settle, but we both know that it will. That's how this works. The world needs balance," he said.

"Have you been listening to Ma'at talk?"

He chuckled. "She makes good points."

"She does. But I'm not interested in them right now." I tucked the scroll into my empty sandals. I'd read it more thoroughly later.

He raised an eyebrow. "And what are you interested in right now?"

"You." I twisted around properly so our faces were only a breath away from one another.

"I can get on board with that conversation."

"It's not a conversation I had in mind," I murmured against his lips.

He threaded his fingers into my hair and tugged my head to him. He kissed me passionately, reminding me why it was his temple I'd agreed to come to.

I melted into him, happy in the knowledge that everything was going to turn out exactly the way I wanted it to.

Eternity didn't seem so long now.

Thank you for reading Thank you for reading Bringer Of The River Waters, I hope you enjoyed it! If you want more from the Forgotten Gods universe, why not try the Forgotten Gods series,

starting with Protectors Of Poison: http://
books2read.com/protectorsofpoison

You can also sign up to my newsletter by
downloading a free Forgotten Gods short story:
https://books.authorlauragreenwood.
co.uk/db2oe9hda9
1

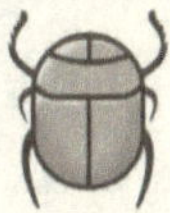

AUTHOR NOTE

Thank you for reading Bringer Of The River Waters, I hope you enjoyed Taweret's story! The events of the stories are based on several different Egyptian myths originating around the New Kingdom. Part of the reason for this is that a lot of Egyptian mythology is contradictory - each region, and even each city, often had a slightly different version of events. This is why some gods and goddesses can be linked to several others. Taweret was first connected to a demon named Apep as her consort, and was an evil figure in mythology, but gradually changed until she became the protective goddess of childbirth, during which time she was often connected as Sobek (and sometimes with other gods). As the other books in the Forgotten Gods: Origins series are based on legends from the

New Kingdom period, that was what I decided to go with for Taweret too.

There are a lot of different myths about how the Nile floods started, and the one about Isis' tears after Osiris died is one of them. In some versions of the myth, Taweret does help her with the aftermath of his death, and in others, she doesn't. I chose this version because I felt it made more sense with the relationship Taweret had built up with Isis' mother (Nut) earlier in the series. (More on family in a moment).

The Wafaa El-Nil festival mentioned has been celebrated since ancient times and lasts for two weeks, starting 15th August - and it's still celebrated today! The Ancient Egyptians believed that the flooding of the Nile occurred when Al-Shaary Al-Yamani (the star, Sirius), appears in the sky.

One of the hardest things about writing about Isis and Osiris (and some of the other gods) is the existence of family ties between them. In the myths, Nut gave birth to Osiris and Isis, as well as Seth and Nephthys, which naturally creates some problems for more modern retellings. However, during my research, I did discover that the ties between Egyptian gods that create families are mostly as a way to group different gods with similar functions together. This is why I decided to make it so that technically, none of them are related by blood at all, though some of them do choose to form family bonds with one another out of affection.

The hippo journey for this book has been a lot of fun too! When I wrote the first scene (with the baby hippo) I was completely certain that hippos can't swim (they can't), but by the time I was writing the scene where Taweret was underwater in her hippo form, I'd started second-guessing myself and ended up on a little bit of a hippo research spiral. And I'm glad I did! Hippos are so amazing to watch underwater, I definitely recommend looking it up if you're interested! One of the other interesting facts I learned is that hippos are actually now extinct in Egypt, despite being numerous in Ancient Times (when Bringer Of The River Waters was set, so that fact couldn't make it into the story).

Shedet, Elephantine, and Karnak, are all real places in Egypt (though sadly, I've only been to one of them, the amazing sights I saw at Karnak temple is one of the reasons that's the main setting for the books in my Forgotten Gods universe.)

And finally, if you missed some of the past events Taweret mentioned in passing, you can find them in the other books in the series - the events that led to Nut giving birth are from Mistress Of Sky And Stars, Thoth and Nehmetawy (the Eye of

Ra) returning from Punt is part of Collector Of Sand And Tears, and Isis and Osiris falling in love is in Queen Of The Two Lands.

Even though Bringer Of The River Waters marks the end of the Forgotten Gods: Origins series (and the stories set in Ancient Times), the Forgotten Gods and The Queen Of Gods series both follow the gods and goddesses of Ancient Egypt but in modern times.

If you want to keep up to date with new releases and other news, you can join my Facebook Reader Group or mailing list.

Stay safe & happy reading!

- Laura

You can find out more about each of my series on my website.

Obscure Academy

A paranormal romance series set at a university-age academy for mixed supernaturals. Each book follows a different couple.

The Apprentice Of Anubis

An urban fantasy series set in an alternative world where the Ancient Egyptian Empire never fell. It follows a new apprentice to the temple of Anubis as she learns about her new role.

Cauldron Coffee Shop

An urban fantasy series following a witch who discovers a cursed warlock living in a teapot.

The Shifter Season

A paranormal Regency romance series following shifters as they attempt to find their match. Each book follows a different couple.

Forgotten Gods

A paranormal adventure romance series inspired by
Egyptian mythology. Each book follows a different
Ancient Egyptian goddess.

Amethyst's Wand Shop Mysteries (with Arizona Tape)

An urban fantasy murder mystery series following a
witch who teams up with a detective to solve murders.
Each book includes a different murder.

Grimm Academy

A fantasy fairy tale academy series. Each book follows a
different fairy tale heroine.

Purple Oasis (with Arizona Tape)

A paranormal romance series based at a sanctuary set up
after the apocalypse. Each book follows a different
couple.

Supernatural Snow Fair

A paranormal romance series based at a
Christmas/winter fair. Each book follows a different
couple.

Speed Dating With The Denizens Of The Underworld
(shared world)

A paranormal romance shared world based on

mythology from around the world. Each book follows a different couple.

Broomstick Bakery

A complete paranormal romance series following a family of witches who run a magical bakery. Each book follows a different couple.

Grimalkin Academy

A complete urban fantasy academy series following a witch cursed to create kittens every time she does magic.

The Paranormal Council

A complete paranormal romance series following paranormals trying to find their fated mates. Each book follows a different couple.

You can find a complete list of all my books on my website:

https://www.authorlauragreenwood.co.uk/p/book-list.html

Signed Paperback & Merchandise:

You can find signed paperbacks, hardcovers, and merchandise based on my series (including stickers, magnets, face masks, and more!) via my website: https://www.authorlauragreenwood.co.uk/p/shop.html

ABOUT LAURA GREENWOOD

Laura is a USA Today Bestselling Author of paranormal, fantasy, urban fantasy, and contemporary romance. When she's not writing, she drinks a lot of tea, tries to resist French macarons, and works towards a diploma in Egyptology. She lives in the UK, where most of her books are set. Laura specialises in quick reads, whether you're looking for a swoonworthy romance for the bath, or an action-packed adventure for your latest journey, you'll find the perfect match amongst her books!

Follow Laura Greenwood

- Website: www.authorlauragreenwood.co.uk
- Mailing List: https://www.authorlauragreenwood.co.uk/p/book-sign-up.html
- Facebook Group: http://facebook.com/groups/theparanormalcouncil

- Facebook Page: http://facebook.com/authorlauragreenwood
- Bookbub: www.bookbub.com/authors/laura-greenwood

www.ingramcontent.com/pod-product-compliance
Lightning Source LLC
Chambersburg PA
CBHW031217160726